RARE BREEDS

By

Erik Hofstatter

Illustrations by Jack Larson

Forward by Paul Kane

DARK
SILO
PRESS

Rare Breeds

Forward by Paul Kane

A couple of years ago I was asked, as I often am, to read some horror fiction with a view to offering a quote. It's one of the things I was very grateful for when I was first starting out and I like to do now, if time allows, with this new generation of writers coming up. It was at this point that I was introduced to Erik Hofstatter's work and was blown away by its boldness. As someone who grew up during the Video Nasty era in the UK, and still has a fondness for all things pulp horror, I very quickly found myself enjoying being dragged along for the ride. Naturally, I was glad to offer a few words to help Erik reach a wider audience, but thought that would be that.

Then a couple of months ago, Erik dropped me another line to tell me he'd done a longer piece of fiction and asked if I'd be willing to do the introduction. Now, understand that at the moment, I am absolutely swamped with work—including three graphic novel scripts, a short novel, a collection and several film projects—but I said sent it along and I'd do one if time allowed. So I dipped in, thinking I'd leave it until I could focus more fully on reading it. But this tale of a sleepwalking husband, his suspicious wife and what happens to their nuclear family already had its hooks into me: just like the Cenobites in my favourite movie of all time.

There are touches of black comedy in this, out and out horror moments, plenty of suspense – not to mention (my particular favourite) a smattering of references to horror movies and TV, like *The Walking Dead* and *Insidious*. There's no better way to appeal to a genre fan like myself. It's a tale of not only forbidden love, but what we'll *do* for love. A story of "what if the past is coming back to haunt us," and a commentary on the breakdown of modern families. In short, Erik writes the kind of old school horror fiction that's rarely seen these days, making him a rare breed himself.

But don't take my word for it, settle back and dive in yourself and you'll see exactly what I mean.

This one's *dead* good…

Paul Kane, March 2015

Acknowledgements

First of all, I would like to thank the legend that is Paul Kane for writing the introduction to this novella. Paul is someone I have tremendous admiration for, so it's needless to say that having his support makes me feel truly blessed. Massive thank you also goes to Mary SanGiovanni and Richard Thomas. Biggest shocker was from Gary McMahon, who was kind enough to offer a blurb for the cover. Again, Gary is a highly respected author (and one of my ultimate idols!) so I'm stunned to have his support, too—a dream come true! Along my writer's journey, I was fortuned to strike a friendship with a fellow horror writer, Karen Runge, who became my trusted beta reader and she helped to shape this work into what it is now. Thank you, Karen, for your diligence and depraved input—ha! I would also like to thank Brian Kaufman for giving me the opportunity to be part of Dark Silo Press and publishing this volume. Last but not least—thank you, dear reader. I hope you'll enjoy this tale that I wove just for you.

Erik Hofstatter, July 2016

1

She slipped out of the satin covers, head groggy from the shifting lunar phase. Thirst clouded her senses, and she failed to notice that he was gone. The bedroom door stood only a few short steps away. Her fingertips brushed against a wall. The surface felt wrinkled and uneven. Zora's sluggish feet navigated through blackness, pivoting on edges of stairs that spiralled into the scanty kitchen. She wiped rheum from the corner of her eyelid, the thick crust crumbling like an anthill. Her face wrinkled with disgust, as she wiped the mucus on a piece of her nightgown.

At the bottom of the stairs, she transitioned from fuzzy carpet to frigid linoleum—the shift in temperature turned her skin into goose flesh. The kitchen reeked of sewage. Patches of dim lustre appeared on the sandstone walls, created by street lamps outside. Plagued with insomnia, she leaned over the sink, peering through the kitchen window and avoiding nasal breaths. The garages were vandalised with graffiti that resembled hieroglyphics. *I swear this town only breeds hooligans and perverts.*

Zora swung the fridge door ajar and grabbed a can of Hobgoblin (*Hemoglobin*, as she'd liked to call it), her preferred brown ale. Air hissed as she cracked the tab open, watching white foam spill around the rim. She gulped beer in frantic draughts, quenching her thirst. *Nothin' like a cold one in the middle of the night!* A beast of a belch sprinted up to her throat, but Zora supressed it.

Then she heard shallow breaths. They echoed from shadows in steady rhythms, out there, tucked in darkness. As she lifted her gaze, the refrigerator light illuminated a static figure of a lanky man, looming next to the appliance. A blank expression was plastered over his sunken façade.

"Fuck!" she said. The red and blue can, sprinkled with condensation, slipped out of her fingers and crashed onto the floor—exploding ale all over the linoleum. Wading through a carob-coloured river of alcohol, she cursed again and pulled a rag from the cupboard under the sink.

"Thanks a lot!" she said. "The kitchen will stink for the rest of the night! I wish you'd stop creeping up on me like this. Yes, we're married now, but I don't know if I'll ever get used to your nightmares." She shook her head.

The man failed to respond. His ape-like arms hung loose by his hips.

Zora knelt, bruising her skin as she cleaned. "Ouch! You should be mopping up this mess, it's your fault!" She flung the rag at him, expecting a catch or some other sign of instinctive reflex. The soaked cloth collided with his worn T-shirt, leaving a stain before falling on the floor. He said nothing—a pillar of silence.

Zora massaged the bridge of her nose. "I'm sorry. You just startled me, that's all. Let's go back to bed." She reached for the man's wrist, guiding him upstairs into the bedroom. The door creaked when Zora nudged it with her shoulder. "Get in there, let me tuck you in."

Like a house built on matchsticks, the man folded onto the mattress. She cuddled next to him, waiting in vain for sleep to take her.

2

He watched as she rolled the barbell away, beads of sweat rolling down her face. Zora worked out constantly, almost fanatical about her body. He had no complaints, and after a year of marriage, he was pretty sure he wouldn't. She was dedicated.

"Want a cuppa?" he asked, standing in the doorway of the spare bedroom they'd refurbished into a home gym.

"No thanks, Sugar," she said, pointing at the plastic shaker she'd filled with protein.

He nodded, flopping down on her oxblood chesterfield sofa and unfolding *The Guardian.* Sunrays penetrated the room, filling the corners with an amber glow.

"I'm just gonna jump in the shower real quick, I smell like camel shit!"

Aurel chuckled. "Never sniffed one myself, but I'll take your word for it." He undressed her with his eyes, and she teased with a cheeky wink. He sipped his morning espresso, flicking through pages. A bantam article captured his attention, and he read the column with profound interest, shaking his head in disbelief.

No, no, not again.

After several minutes passed, the bathroom door creaked open and unleashed a cloud of steam into the narrow corridor. Zora emerged, towel wrapped around her head like a turban. She leaned over him, investigating what he was reading.

"The grave-robbing story? I glanced at that this morning. Shocking, isn't it? Why would someone desecrate a grave like that? Do you think they fuck the body? Like, what do you call them?" She said, clicking her fingers.

"Necrophiliacs?"

"That's the one!" Zora said, pilfering her husband's coffee. Apparently, it was a child's grave that they robbed. That's even more bizarre. What kind of person steals a corpse of a child?"

"A demented one. But this is Chatham, where anything goes," he said, tossing the papers aside and avoiding her gaze. The morbid topic invoked nausea within him. Zora noticed his nervous twitching and decided to change the subject.

"Hey! Guess what? A zombie broke into our kitchen again last night," she began, slapping his thigh with gusto.

Aurel rolled his eyes, sheepish. "Shit! I'm really sorry. I don't remember any of it."

"You never do, Sugar."

"What happened?"

She snuggled into Aurel's lap, stroking his dark ash hair.

"I woke up and went down to the kitchen to grab a beer. You must've wandered off at some point during the night, and I found you by accident— guarding the fridge. You just stood there, staring into nothing. It freaked me out! I dropped my beer, spilling it everywhere. I know that I should be used to it by now, but the strange thing was, I didn't even hear you get out of bed. You walk, or should I say *float*, like a bloody ghost!"

"At least I didn't attempt a night drive this time," he said, grinning.

"Thank God for that!"

Her fingers slithered down to his cheeks.

"What are you thinking about?" she asked.

"Nothing important,"

"You don't have to feel embarrassed about your affliction. I told you that before."

"I know, but it's important that you understand." He brushed her hand aside and rose from the sofa.

"Understand what?"

"That this thing is beyond my control."

"Of course I understand. I married you, didn't I? I knew what I was getting myself into. Yes, your walks are hard to cope with sometimes, but you don't do it every night. No one's perfect. We all have our little quirks."

He rubbed a finger alongside his nose. "Yeah, don't I know it!"

3

Aurel paced along the street, his nimble feet eluding puddles. He entered Capstone valley, a former farm converted into a landscaped park. On Sundays, the lake swarmed with anglers, sporting silly, outback-style hats. Aurel stopped to watch. A pasty-looking boy with freckles emerged from a fishing tent, passing a steaming thermos to the man next to him. Their lips moved, and their faces cracked into grins. The boy took a slice of bread from a plastic sack, tearing it into pieces, hurling chunks into the lake. Ducks converged on the bread, quacking and flapping. Aurel sighed and shook his head.

Leaving the families behind, he resumed his walk at a slower pace. A fox greeted him from a remote coppice as he crossed Maze Wood. The scent of chestnuts lingered in the air. The park stretched over 114 hectares of land, divided into ancient woodland blocks. He travelled a shamrock green field in search of the hidden path that led to the river. Glancing back, he saw the fox, alone on the rim of the wood.

"Where's your family?" he whispered. As if the fox could hear, it turned and ducked into the brush.

He evaded a protruding branch and slipped on the steep crosscut—plummeting into mud and bruising his coccyx.

Bollocks! Now it looks like I shat myself.

He sprang up with childish embarrassment and lumbered through the underbrush. Gusts of wind rustled in the trees, and a blackcap flew above. Aurel sniffed at his palms, curious, praying that the sticky sludge was truly mud and not dog shit. Concern satisfied, he marched on. The path divided and he hesitated. *I don't have to do this. I can just turn around now and go home. Oh, but I need to see her. I must see her!*

The foliage blocked out the sun, casting a cloak of shadows around his shoulders. A darkened path sloped down, hurrying him along. Compost fused with moisture persisted in the atmosphere. A swinging duo of branches concealed an arch-shaped tunnel, leading deep into the ground. The cave resembled a war bunker. He halted, inspecting the entrance to the sanctuary that sheltered him from all the cruelties of the world. It served as a getaway to another realm, one where he did not need to pretend. Inside the tunnel, felicity reigned supreme. A colossal chain with a digital padlock guarded the wicket. The device beeped as Aurel hit a series of digits.

All these years and my knees are still trembling.

Yanking the barrier open required a Herculean effort. Aurel seized the handles, jerking and pulling. A speck of perspiration dampened his brow. The gate screeched and a putrid smell assaulted him. Aurel eyeballed the darkness within, dueling with an insatiable appetite. Powerless to resist, he stepped inside.

4

He returned home in time for lunch. The abhorrent aroma of tofu persisted in the house. Zora—a devout vegan—chose to consume a string of truly revolting dishes, and in his opinion, tofu was the foulest.

"But it's healthy!" she said.

Aurel wriggled his nose. "It doesn't *smell* healthy. It's like chewing an eyeball. The consistency is all slimy on top and gooey in the middle."

"You're such a drama queen, worse than Livie! I'll feed this to you as a punishment, whenever you piss me off."

Today was *that* day.

He scrubbed mud off his boots on the doormat. "Hey! Sorry I'm late! How's it going?"

Zora stirred her culinary creation with vigour. "Fine, thanks. Did you manage to tie up your loose end?"

"Yep, all sorted."

The way she flexed her jaw muscles indicated anger, and he attempted to lighten up the mood. "What's for lunch, dear? I could eat a dolphin!"

She pierced him with a glare, eyes like javelins. Zora supported animal conservation.

They both idolized David Attenborough, but for conflicting reasons. To her, he was a wildlife legend. But to him—a cure for insomnia.

"Your absolute favourite! Tofu!" she said, sarcasm dripping from her words. "Livie? Lunch is ready!" Her voice soared to disturbing levels, like a soprano's, and penetrated the very back of Aurel's skull. He collapsed into a chair. He closed his eyes and massaged his temples.

Zora's ten-year-old daughter descended from her lair, face covered in white powder. Her eyes were smeared with eyeliner and lips decorated with onyx lipstick. He grimaced in shock.

"Is it Halloween already?"

She smirked, veering around and bolting back upstairs.

"Livie! What about lunch?" Zora said.

The door slammed with a thunderous bang.

Zora sighed, tossing a dishcloth in the sink. "Thanks a lot."

"What? You okay with her Jack Sparrow tribute?" Aurel asked, scooping a mouthful of tofu from the crystal bowl, avoiding thoughts of eyeballs.

"She's just playing. You'd know this if you had kids of your own."

Aurel clenched his fist. "Maybe you should give me one, then."

"I'm not having this discussion again. I'm too old to have a child with you."

"But not too old to have one with someone else, eh?"

"If you wanted a kid so badly you should've married some young slapper, instead of a forty-one-year old divorcee!"

He nodded, contemplating in silence.

Zora groaned. "Look, I'm sorry. I shouldn't have said that. You're a great father to Livie and she loves you," she said, stroking his hand.

"And I love her like my own. It's just...you know how obsessed my mother is with me starting a family."

"We *are* your family, silly."

"I know, I know. Come here," he said, pulling her closer. They snogged in a half-seated embrace. The scent of butterscotch shampoo still lingered in her hair.

5

She cradled his testicles like a pair of Baoding balls, her fingers slithering up and clasping his shaft. It stiffened in her grasp as she stroked in steady rhythm. Aurel lay on his back, a moaning plank in the darkness. He flipped his wife over, sliding two fingers into the moist slit between her legs before penetrating with urgency.

But the sex lacked passion. It bored him. He was forced to think of Cornelia with each thrust, just to sustain his erection. Zora's bouncing breast brushed against his forearm as he withdrew his cock, spraying a sperm lagoon into her navel. The whole process was over in seconds.

* * * * *

The bedroom's humid air tasted stale as she rolled with the duvet. Aurel farted in his sleep, oblivious. A burning sensation pressed against her bladder and she groaned with frustration. Yielding to the restless voices in her head, Zora crept into the downstairs bathroom.

On the cold toilet seat, goose bumps stippled her milky thighs as she waited for nature to run its course. Zora flushed and strolled into the kitchen, flicking the light switch on. She liberated another can of Hobgoblin from the fridge. It seemed that this had become a habit. The malty taste of cold ale refreshed her as she leaned against the sink, gulping. She glanced at the artwork on the container, which depicted an axe-wielding goblin with quiver of arrows and a mischievous grin. After another swig, she returned to the bedroom.

I really ought to change jobs. Night shifts are seriously fucking up my body clock. I can't remember the last time I got some decent shuteye. The job itself changed so much, I'm not even sure I enjoy it anymore. Greedy corporate cunts! Grinding people down and replacing them like bog rolls!

She slammed into bed, and then realized she might have woken him. No reason for her frustration with her job to ruin his night's sleep. She rolled over to spoon him.

He was gone.

Bugger! He must've wandered off again! We really need to talk about this. Whatever the fuck is wrong—it needs to stop!

She flew out of bed and bolted down the spiral stairs. The kitchen was empty and still whiffed of ale. The living room was empty, too. No trace of him in the bathroom. Zora sprinted outside and peered at the garage—it was locked. Only one more room remained. Her grip tightened around the knob, twisting. Hinges creaked as she stepped inside, holding breath in anticipation. At first, the room appeared undisturbed.

Livie mumbled in her sleep, pulling at the quilt. Moonlight illuminated the peaceful silhouette of Zora's daughter as she stroked her tawny hair. Then she saw a glimmer of silver. Zora shrieked at the shadowed figure that towered over Livie's bed, facing the wall—blade in hand. Zora's pulse throbbed so fast that she feared her heart would rupture. She tiptoed towards him, slipping the blade out of her husband's grasp.

Ambivalent feelings raged inside her. Fear versus anger. Love versus hate. She tightened her grip on the knife, wrestling with maternal instincts that forced her to point the tip at his ribs, and shield Livie at all cost. Zora considered scooping her from the bed and rush her to safety. But then what? How would she explain this nightmarish situation to a ten-year-old? No, she had to get Aurel out of the room.

Trembling with fury, she clasped his wrist and dragged him out. He complied, his steps slow and drowsy. She gazed into his eyes. They flickered in rapid motion. *What in the bleeding hell is going on in that weird brain of yours?* Aurel's limbs stiffened, his mouth muttering incoherent sentences. He slipped out of her grip, shambling back upstairs while she followed behind in dead silence.

6

The afternoon sun pierced her eyelids as she jerked awake, gasping for oxygen. Dark circles of perspiration stained her nightgown. She peeled the cold fabric off her stomach, then tossed it aside. Aurel's embroidered bathrobe hung on the door and she slipped into it. He reclined on the sofa as Zora descended from the room above. She approached, jaw clenched and seething with anger, hurt and worry.

"Hi, love! How'd you sleep?"

"We need to talk," she said, snatching the remote out of his hand. "You were sleepwalking again last night. We've talked about your theories before, but that seemed like it was for fun. I never actually took the discussion seriously. Now I have to ask, do you think your obsession with astral projection might be connected to your sleepwalking?"

Aurel produced one of his rare smiles, flashing his crooked teeth. "Have you been watching *Insidious* again?"

"I'm serious. What exactly is it? We need to get to the bottom of this."

He inhaled with drama. "We've discussed it before!"

"Well, I wasn't paying attention. Tell me again."

"Fine. Feel free to take notes this time. In a nutshell, it's an out of body experience. You basically assume the existence of an *astral body* that leaves your *physical* body, allowing you to travel outside of it in astral plane. There's an Amazon tribe, the Yaskomo of the Waiwai, who believe in performing a *soul flight*. They fly to the sky and consult cosmological beings. These kind of beliefs vary from culture to culture, of course."

"And what's in this astral plane?"

"It's a world of celestial spheres populated by angels, spirits, and other immaterial beings. The soul crosses through in its astral body on the way to being born and after death."

"That's ridiculous. I didn't pass though anything when I was born, except my mother's vagina."

"Hey! Don't piss on my beliefs! There's more to it, but I can see you're a sceptic so I'll get to the point. No, I'm not astral projecting. I'm merely sleepwalking."

She tucked a strand of hair behind her ear. "Okay, if you say so. The reason I'm asking is because something terrible happened last night. Something that has never happened before. When I noticed you were out of bed, I ran into the kitchen then bathroom even the garage—I searched everywhere." Zora paused, attempting to stop her voice from shaking, "I eventually found you in Livie's room. With a knife."

Melancholy polluted the air around them. Zora studied her husband's shiny complexion; he appeared lifeless, almost like a wax figure.

He met her gaze, stuttering. "I'm s-sorry...I don't remember anything!"

She clasped his hand in hers.

"It's alright, Sugar. It's not your fault that you're ill," she said, but the lie reflected in her voice. "You really need to see a doctor about this, though. I can book an appointment for you, if you like. The sleepwalking is getting worse and sooner or later you could hurt someone." She made her case in the sweetest tone she could muster.

Aurel nodded, face blank. "Yes, you're absolutely right, but I would never hurt you or Livie—not consciously anyway." He gave her a slight grin, but dropped it when Zora's expression remained solemn.

"I don't know why it happens. Sleepwalking generally consists of repeated behaviours—an automatism, so to speak, and I've never displayed any violent urges before. I tell you what, let's keep this to ourselves for now, and I swear to you on Livie's life that if it ever happens again, I'll see a doctor and get myself a nice cocktail of drugs, yeah?"

She shook her head. "That's not good enough. Don't you get it? *I fear for you both!* I love you and don't want this marriage to crumble, but you need help. I'm so torn! I don't know whether to lash at you, or comfort you, or what! But one thing is certain, I can't let you endanger my daughter's life again. Think about what would've happened if I hadn't found you in time."

"Nothing would've happened. I would've probably turned around after a few minutes and walked back upstairs. I'm *sleep-walking* not *sleep-stabbing*! And even if I was astral projecting—it's harmless. Trust me."

* * * * *

Aurel's thoughts belied his outward calm. *I needed the flippin' knife! You must protect yourself in the astral world in case of confrontation. If an entity finds you, digs its nails into you... argh, if only you knew.*

"And what if you started slicing *my* daughter like a pig on a spit! Don't look at me like that! You need to face up to your responsibilities like a man! Next time it might be too late. Someone could end up dead!"

"You're just paranoid," he replied, avoiding her eyes by shifting his gaze towards the electric fire. The dancing flames relaxed him for a split second, but he struggled to control his silent rage.

"No, I'm not! Stop being so selfish! You need to deal with this now! You need help! Do you hear me?"

Aurel sprang from the sofa, pacing back and forth. He hoped his body language would demonstrate that he was taking her seriously. "You're right," he said. "I know a specialist, and I'm going to make an appointment, okay?"

She bit her lower lip and considered his words. "When?"

When it happens again, he thought.

7

When he exited the house, the sky was dull and grey. Only a short drive away, the gravel crunched under the tyres of the family Chrysler, as he pulled into Capstone Valley car park. The early morning was desolate. Aurel strolled along the lakeshore, watching mist settle over the marshlands like drops of impending doom. Entering the Orchid Wood, he turned to the side, sliding down the hidden path. A limb from an ancient oak swooshed above his head. The tunnel, masked by branches, was three metres in front. He uncoiled the chain. The muscles in his forearms flexed as he swung the gate open with a grunt. The crisp air burned his nasal passage, as he inhaled fresh oxygen one last time. Then he stepped inside the putrid tunnel.

Aurel patted around in the dark, locating his light source within seconds. He switched on the flashlight and closed the gate behind him. Shadows crept along the stained walls as he edged forward. Disgusted by the morbid aroma,

he pinched his nose. Candlelight shone from a compact opening in the east wall, where several bricks were missing. He approached it with caution.

"Cornelia? Are you in here?" he whispered into the passage. A soft clunk echoed from within, as if a hammer or a tool of some kind had been dropped. He waited.

At last, an ethereal figure clad in white emerged from the tiny hole in the wall. She was petite, with a delicate nose and a generous mouth. Her oval face radiated beauty, and Aurel gasped at the celestial sight of her. How did she manage to stay so clean in a place like this? So fresh? So mouth-watering?

"You just can't get enough of me, can you?" she said.

Aurel dropped his gaze.

"Ah, I see. You're still ashamed even after all these years," she said. The woman crept closer. She lifted his chin with a knuckle, planting a hungry kiss. He hesitated at first, but soon relaxed and their tongues fought like dueling cobras.

She slipped her hand into his, fingers entwined, and led him inside her lair. The chamber was miniscule but cozy. He overstepped a mummified cadaver of a tween girl, and the pair fell on the mattress together in a savage embrace. They made love with vigorous passion. After the deed, Aurel's head rested on the woman's chest, whilst she stroked his back, soaked with sweat. Time ceased to exist when they were cocooned together.

"This can't continue, Cornelia. I have a family," said Aurel, breaking the golden silence.

"They're *not* your family! *I am!*" Cornelia said, sliding his head away from her breasts.

Aurel met her hypnotic eyes—eyes that resembled his. It was like looking at his own reflection. "I love Zora,"

"More than you love me?"

"It's a different kind of love. Society would never accept what we are!"

"Fuck society and their political correctness!" Cornelia spat. "Pharaohs in Ancient Egypt married their siblings and had children with them. Various combinations of relations were practiced among royalty as a means of perpetuating the royal lineage."

"But we're not in Ancient Egypt and you're not a royal! You live in a fucking filthy hole in the ground like *Bilbo Baggins*!"

"Keep your voice down! You're missing my point, brother. I'm asking why should we be ashamed and condemned for our love by modern society when it was perfectly natural hundreds of years ago? Why was it acceptable then but not now? Who decides what's acceptable? One cretin proclaims it unnatural and the rest of the sheep follow. Fuck them, I say. We should pity them."

"You're wrong." Aurel shook his head in disagreement. "Do you remember what we did together in that tunnel when we were children? How traumatised I was? This is all your fault!"

"Fine. I'll play the villain, if it makes you feel better. It was most unfortunate that you witnessed one of my experiments so early on, but it would've never happened if you didn't follow me into the tunnel in the first place."

"You're evil!" Aurel moaned. "You always were. What you did to that poor girl...have you been doing it for all these years? Have you read the papers I brought you? That was you, wasn't it? Why am I even asking this question? Is this her? The one from the papers?" Aurel tapped the mummified corpse of the little girl with his foot.

Cornelia shoved him aside. "Don't touch her! She doesn't like it!"

"And how do you know that? Did she tell you? Can you communicate with the dead now? Why are you doing this?"

"I was waiting for science to find ways for this girl to live again," Cornelia sobbed. "I wanted to communicate with her. I lay on the grave and tried to get in touch with her. I listened to what she said. Often, she asked me to take her on a walk."

Aurel listened to Cornelia's ravings with compassion. He glanced at the mummified girl. At the striped stockings, knee lengths boots—her lips smeared with red lipstick. She almost resembled a doll.

"I put a music box in her ribcage too. Listen, Aurel." She squeezed the corpse's ribs and a melody played.

He stood there, slack-jawed and afraid. "This isn't happening. You're not human!"

Cornelia pierced her brother with a murderous glare. "Why do you keep coming back then? Hmm? I tell you why—because you can't live without me! And do you know why you can't live without me? *Because you and I are the same!* I am you, Aurel, and you are me! You crave what I crave! This excites you as much as it excites me!"

"I'm nothing like you!" Aurel said. He dressed himself and exited the chamber.

The woman followed his footsteps in the dark until they reached the end of the tunnel. "You'll be back," she said with a self-assured smirk.

Aurel shouted down the tunnel before shutting the gate. "You're wrong this time, Sister. I'm not coming back. I'm not sick like you."

Yes, you are, dear brother. You'll be back soon enough. Soon you'll realize that we belong together, that we were destined to be together. Fuck the rest of the world and their pathetic views. And if you won't come to me, I'll come to you...

8

The heavens unleashed a devastating storm that night. Aurel lazed on the sofa, balancing a laptop on his loin—the heat radiating from its battery spread into his thighs. He could hear Zora groaning from the home gym. She'd discovered a new fitness regimen called *CrossFit* that kept her busy on most evenings.

He glared at the blank Google search box, sipping a glass of whisky. His fingertips itched to type in the word, the word that had haunted him for days. Aurel shut his eyes, letting memories transport him back to childhood.

He was twelve when he first caught his sister in the act. Cornelia had begun to display symptoms of disturbing behaviour. Aurel witnessed her dissecting a frog once, long before she progressed on to larger animals. She must've got tired of amphibians but as far as he recalled, she never showed any interest in humans. People bored her.

They used to dare each other to climb over the cemetery gates at midnight, walk to the farthest grave, touch it, and *walk*—not run—

back to the entrance. Cornelia always won. She seemed comfortable in the presence of the dead, even at that early age. One night, she did not return. He waited for an hour outside the gates before rousing their father, Alexander, in panic.

Soon after that, a body vanished. Someone had dug it up and stolen it. Aurel suspected Cornelia. He kept an eye on his sister for the next few weeks.

She chose her hideout well and remained vigilant, but Aurel followed her inside the tunnel when she bunked school one sunny afternoon. What began as a spot for Cornelia's perverted desires eventually turned into a permanent lair.

When he entered the tunnel for the first time, he was unprepared for what he was about to see. Cornelia knelt beside the puny body of a girl...embalming her.

He screamed, wanting to run, but fear paralyzed his legs. He couldn't move. Cornelia traipsed over to him. "Come and help me, brother," she said. Aurel collapsed to the ground, observing in monastic silence until he finally joined her, handing over various instruments. When she finished with her 'art,' Cornelia crawled next to him.

"Let's masturbate together," she said.

Aurel gasped in shock. Sexual experimentation seemed quite common amongst kids in puberty—but with his own twin sister?

Her hand snaked onto his crotch and began to caress it. Aurel flinched, but his twin held a strange dominance over him. He could not resist. What began as a harmless experiment between siblings quickly escalated into vigorous lovemaking.

They left the tunnel and strolled towards home. Cornelia beamed with satisfaction, but

Aurel's shoulders twitched under the weight of sin. The traumatic experience burned scars into his soul.

Cornelia ran away from home shortly after the coitus. Their parents were devastated by her disappearance, but never reported her missing. Aurel presumed she lived in that awful tunnel with her precious mummies, thriving amongst the dead. And that's where he left her—in solitude for decades.

Until he met Zora.

When Zora enquired about his family, Aurel explained that his father had died from a heart attack, and that his relationship with his mother was complicated.

"Any brothers or sisters?" Zora said.

"No, I'm an only child."

He yearned to start his own family, a *normal* family.

Over the years, Cornelia wrote letters, declaring her eternal love, hinting she was closer than he thought. He suspected she'd found another tunnel—near their house—but suppressed the thought.

Then fate intervened. One bleak, cold morning, Zora invited her sister, Karen, over for coffee.

Zora lurked behind a curtain, peering at passing cars, and mumbling beneath her breath. "She's late!"

Aurel lounged on the sofa, reading the papers with poor concentration—the words eluding him. Interacting with new people was a challenge he tried to avoid. A small, snot-coloured car pulled up outside their window.

"Karen's here! She's finally here!" Zora said, bouncing with excitement.

She swung the door open, revealing a charismatic young woman clad in black. Her oval face was pale like the moon, her plump lips decorated with a ruby red lipstick. Aurel gazed into her eyes, big and bright, and emanating intelligence. Strands of raven black hair dangled over her delicate shoulders.

"Come here, you! I haven't seen you in ages!" Zora said.

When Zora and her sister embraced, Aurel felt a stunned rush of memories. That one display of sibling affection brought it all back. Aurel wept. He loved Cornelia, despite her perversions.

When he married Zora, they moved together into the city and he decided to tour local tunnels—searching for his estranged twin. An abandoned bunker lay near their property, and intuition suggested that's where he'd find her. The entrance remained unlocked back then. He wrapped a chain around the gate in a feeble attempt to stop her cravings. More corpses continued to disappear, and he suspected that she'd discovered another route.

In the beginning, Aurel lacked courage to enter the hideout. The traumatic memories of his childhood felt fresh, even after all those years. He veered around at the threshold, but her melodic voice pulled him in. "I knew you would come back to me one day," she said.

He bowed his head, defeated and embarrassed. Words failed him. Cornelia cupped his cheek, "It's all right, brother."

Aurel explained about Zora and her beautiful daughter, Livie. Cornelia listened with interest and fascination.

"Well, my younger brother is now a stepfather, eh? I hope you'll be a better one than that bastard who fathered us," she said, spitting out a ball of phlegm.

"Mummies? What you looking at them for?"

The voice startled him. Aurel snapped from his reverie. The perplexed face of Livie loomed over his shoulder. He *did* type the word into the search box without realizing. Multiple images of embalmed bodies were displayed on the screen.

"What?"

"Why are you looking at mummies?" Livie said.

He slammed the laptop shut with unnecessary force. "We just had an interesting debate about mummification with a colleague at work today, that's all."

She spun around, skipping away from him. "*Whatever.* You're sick."

9

She returned to work that night, and Aurel plundered the fridge in her absence. A six-pack of Hobgoblin grinned at him, but he knew better than to steal Zora's ale. Half a bottle of Isle of Jura whiskey waited in the cabinet, and he poured himself a generous glass.

Aurel strolled towards Livie's room—glass in hand, the amber liquid whispering words of encouragement. *I need to make more of an effort. I hardly talk to the kid.* He was on the verge of knocking, but the high-pitched screams blaring through the door stopped him. Livie mentioned something about *Cradle of Pink* being her latest favourite band. No, *Cradle of Filth*—that was it! The "music" sounded like a cat being strangled. Aurel swallowed another mouthful of whiskey, waiting.

* * * * *

Behind the closed door, Livie (her tastes far more ghoulish than most girls in her class) sat behind a desk—flipping through Francisco Goya's "Black Paintings," admiring one painting in particular—*Saturn Devouring His Son.* This fascinating piece depicted the Greek myth of the Titan Cronus, who feared that he would be overthrown by one of his children so he ate each one upon their birth. She gazed at his teeth, ripping off the infant's arm, and admiring the rich colour of the flesh.

Goya's biography intrigued her. He began as a boring court painter for the Spanish Crown, painting romantic portraits and such, before going deaf and buying an abandoned house called *Quinda del Sordo* (aptly translated as 'The Deaf Man's House.")

In this residence, he began painting darker subjects on canvas and on walls of the house itself. The story goes that he never intended for the paintings to be exhibited. He did not write of them, and most likely never spoke of them. They were only discovered some fifty years later after his death and transferred to canvas support. Goya completed work on his fourteen Black Paintings at the age of seventy-five, alone and in serious physical decline.

* * * * *

Aurel shook his head, choosing not to knock after all. The obscene noise decided him. He veered around and strolled back into the living room—seeking the serenity of the sofa. The sofa obliterated his worries. Or was that the whiskey? He stretched and shut his eyes, allowing the naked images of Cornelia to wash over him. Her words echoed through the hollow caves of his mind.

You crave what I crave! This excites you as much as it excites me!

He drained the glass and poured himself another. The potent liquid coursed through his veins, drowning him in oblivion. Aurel gazed at the ceiling, fascinated. The pecan-coloured stains reminded him of something or someone. He tilted his head to the side. *Ah, yes! Jesus on the cross!* He chuckled and risked one more sip. Wrapped up in drunken thoughts, he failed to register the gentle tapping on the window glass. The Morse code tapping like sound continued until he propped up—disorientated. *What the fuck is that? Did Zora forget something?*

Aurel staggered towards the window with a glass of whiskey, smiling at the raging liquid inside. He peered at the dim surface of the window but saw nothing except his own drunken reflection. *This stuff is stronger than Hercules! It's melting my brain!* The sofa whispered to him from afar, and he obeyed, stumbling closer. Then the tapping resumed. Someone was outside, demanding his attention.

He flipped the switch off, bathing in darkness. When he glimpsed the figure outside, the glass slipped from his trembling fingers.

Cornelia. Soaked to the bone—waiting. Watching. The rain poured over her, yet that seraphic glow refused to be washed away. Aurel noticed a minor smudge of dirt above her left breast. It angered him for elusive reasons. Cornelia knocked and knocked with a child-like grin. Furious, Aurel swung the door open— ushering her inside.

"What the fuck are you doing here? Are you insane?"

Cornelia tilted her head to one side, pondering the question. "Relax, dear brother. I waited till your wifey was gone. Glorious weather for an evening stroll, don't you think?"

"Shut up! I have a stepdaughter too, remember? She's in her room, right now!" He dragged Cornelia by her arm inside the home-gym, slamming the door behind them. "You dare come into my house? What were you thinking? How do you even know where we live?"

"That's nasty!" Cornelia said, pointing at the stained ceiling: "Look, there's a bit of damp in the corner there. You might want to do something about that, too."

"You live in a tunnel. What the fuck do you know?"

Cornelia chuckled. "You're right of course, but it has its perks—I don't have to worry about a mortgage like you do."

"This is not the time for jokes. You can't be here! How did you find us?"

Cornelia leaned against Zora's incline bench, crossing her frail arms. "It's a small world. I visited mother years ago. She gladly revealed your whereabouts when I applied the right amount of pressure. I kept my eye on you ever since, wondering, dreaming, and hoping that one day you would come back to me. I changed my location from time to time, because I wanted to remain close to you."

He swallowed, words sticking in his throat. Aurel loathed this fucking city. When they married, he spent months convincing Zora to move up north. Somewhere quiet and isolated, where trees outnumbered people—but uprooting Livie was out of the question.

"I can't deny it," he confessed. "Having you so close showers me with happiness. You are my sister, after all, and I love you more than words can show."

"I'm sure there's another way you can show how much you love me," Cornelia teased with a mischievous grin, slowly unbuttoning her drenched dress.

Aurel flushed with embarrassment and something else.

Lust.

"You have to go!" he said. "I promise I'll come and see you soon, but we have to be careful. Zora's suspicions are growing. We can't do it here!"

She sprang from the bench and into her brother's embrace. "Stop panicking. You know you can't resist me," she said, licking his lips with a wet tongue.

He took the bait, surrendering to Cornelia's touch. His twin moaned as he nibbled at her exposed breast—goading her nipple with a cheeky bite. She felt his cock grow in her grasp. When he rubbed her clit, Cornelia crumbled on the floor. Aurel spread her legs and she licked his fingers, guiding them inside her—two, then three. Her body quaked as she stroked her brother's shaft.

Perhaps it was the booze, or the sex, or the combination of both that made him forget. The gym's door had a busted lock that failed to shut. That's why he could hear Zora's workouts. Lost in passion, he never saw the eye peeking through the gap. Barely breathing, Livie witnessed everything.

10

They dined together before Zora left for her night job. The menu featured risotto. The rice tasted bland and rigid, a result of undercooking. Still, it delighted Aurel. Evenings without tofu had to be cherished.

Livie barely touched her plate. She asked to be excused and retreated back to her crypt.

"What's wrong with her?" he asked.

"I don't know, she's been quiet for the last few days," Zora said between mouthfuls.

He nodded, pondering the cause of his stepdaughter's mysterious withdrawal. "Did she get her first period or something?"

She raised an eyebrow.

Aurel dreaded Zora's cycles, as she often transformed into an ogress. One minute she was koala-hugging him, the next she was a praying mantis. He hoped that the trait wasn't hereditary. "I could talk to her," he offered.

"You're welcome to try. I gotta go."

Aurel accompanied his wife to the door and brushed her lips with a kiss. "See you in the morning, darling," he said.

"Have fun."

＊ ＊ ＊ ＊ ＊

Aurel knocked and entered. Livie sat cross-legged on her bed, head buried in her iPhone.

"Whatcha doing?"

"What does it look like?" she said, eyes on the screen.

He sat on the edge of the bed, the mattress protesting under his weight. "We're worried about you, sweet pea. Your mum told me you've been very quiet lately. Any particular reason? Anything you wanna share?"

Livie stopped typing, but still failed to meet his gaze. "I don't want to talk about it. Not with you. Just leave me alone."

Don't lose your temper. His lip curled into a retarded grin. "What's the matter, hon? Are you having boy problems? Whatever it is, you can tell me."

She dropped the phone and buried her face in the pillow. Then she erupted like Mount Edna. "I *saw* you, alright!"

Aurel flinched, stunned by the explosion. "You saw what, sweet pea?"

Her voice broke, tears welling up in the corners of her eyes. "I saw you drunk...in the gym," she sobbed, "and I saw what you were doing..."

Blood drained from his face and the whole room spun. "I...it's complicated," he mumbled, more to himself than her. "You can't tell you mother! It would hurt her very much."

Livie scowled, a stream of black eyeliner staining her pink cheeks.

Aurel reached for her knee but she pulled away.

"Leave me alone now. Please!" she said.

His mind raced—digging for possible explanations. Surely he could outwit a ten-year old? "Honey...it's not what you think."

Livie met his gaze then. Fires of defiance burned in her cobalt-blue eyes, reminding Aurel of an oilrig fire. The way flames burn on the blue surface of the horizon. Sad, but beautiful.

"It's *exactly* what I think. I know what I saw."

He scratched under his armpit, patting a moist patch. "I can explain if you give me a chance."

She turned away from him. "There's no way I'm going to talk about this with you. I won't tell, okay? But I can't talk about this."

Aurel gazed at his stepdaughter's back, his face twitching from the stabs of pain and panic. Could he trust a child with a secret he'd guarded for so many years? "I love you," he said, his voice trembling. Humiliated, Aurel plodded back to the sofa. His mind was a jumble, plagued with questions of his future happiness.

I can't trust a fucking child with something like this. She's going to tell. I know she will. Fuck! We've been careful all this time. One small blunder, and it all falls like a game of dominoes. No, I can't leave my happiness in her hands. I need a guarantee that she will keep quiet. But how? How can I keep her mouth shut?

* * * * *

Morpheus entered Livie's dreams that night in the guise of her stepfather. Aurel was dressed in a scarlet robe, wielding a blade and creeping ever closer to her bed. Rivers of blood swallowed all in the next fragment of her nightmare. She sprang up, panting, and drenched in sweat. Livie peered into the darkness, her eyes inspecting every corner. She struggled to control her frantic breathing.

She was reminded of an incident when her mother first married him. She slept in their bed, wedged between them, when she was roused by a sudden urge to pee.

Returning from the bathroom, the sight of a full moon caught her eye, and she gazed at it from the window for a briefest of moments. Then she turned back to bed and gasped. Aurel's sleeping body planked up halfway, his head shifted in her direction—glaring. She felt her own body grow stiff, assuming she'd done something wrong.

"Did you take the cake out of the oven?"

Livie blinked, confused.

"What did you say?"

"Ahhh," he groaned, slamming his body back on the mattress—fast asleep.

The episode frightened her beyond reason, and she hadn't slept in their bed since. The next morning, she tried to talk to Zora. "Aurel is a sleepwalker, darling, remember?" she'd explained. "There's nothing to worry about. If it happens again, just wake me and I'll take care of him."

Livie shook off the memory and wiped sweat off her brow. Sleep proved elusive for the rest of the night.

11

Aurel was not a morning person. He only envied one aspect of Zora's night job—she did not have to rise early. The toasty duvet had its claws in him, refusing to let go. He lazed until the last minute, and then willed himself to get up. He promised to make Livie pancakes for breakfast. The kitchen was quiet when he descended the stairs, mumbling under his breath. Livie usually rose at the crack of dawn, eager to paint her face on and straighten her hair.

He put the kettle on and plodded to her bedroom. The closed door struck him as odd. "Time to get up, princess. I'll start making your pancakes in a minute," he said, knocking.

No reply, so he tried again. "Livie? Are you dressed? I'm coming in,"

Aurel gasped. Not at the vacant bed, but at the stiff body lying on the carpet. Livie's hair was matted to her forehead, soaked in sweat. Her face was white as bone. He fell to his knees—pressing on her haemorrhaging stomach with bloodstained hands. Surveying the room, he snatched a towel from a nearby chair to pressurize the wound.

Oh, my God! What happened to her? Why is she bleeding so much?

The geyser of blood flowed from the gash and he realized that Livie had been stabbed.

No, no, no! How did this happen? It wasn't me! Why can't I remember anything? I have to get her to a hospital! He snatched the car keys from the shelf and opened the door. Then he scooped her frail body, glancing at the pale flesh painted red. He whisked her to the car, legs wobbly.

If she dies, Zora will never forgive me!

The leather squeaked as he slid her figure on the backseat. He climbed in and ignited the engine. The Chrysler roared, and Aurel's foot hit the accelerator—burning rubber with a screech. He raced down the road, swerving past traffic. Honks echoed behind him. A double-decker bus pulled out, and he avoided collision by a fraction. He glanced in the rear-view mirror—Livie's body was fading to grey with every passing minute. His heart raced faster than the car.

Maybe it's too late. What if she's dead already? What am I going to do? What am I going to say to Zora? Wish I could remember what happened. Did I really stab her?

Aurel whipped out his Sony Xperia and dialed Zora's number. He pressed the phone to his ear, the other hand firm on the steering wheel. Calling whilst driving was the least of his problems.

"Hey, Sugar! What's up?" she said on the other end of the line.

Aurel cleared his throat in an attempt to conceal the distress in his voice. "Morning. It's Livie…she had a little accident."

"What? What happened?"

"Oh don't worry, it's nothing serious. I slept over and she came up to wake me. She slipped on the stairs and sprained her ankle. I'm taking her to Maritime Hospital now. Just wanted to let you know so you're not worried when you get home from work and we're not there."

"Aww, bless her! She's so clumsy. I'm finishing in half an hour. Want me to drive straight to the hospital and meet you there?"

Panicking, he was grateful that Zora could not see his face. "From Ashford? After a night shift? No, it'll take ages and you're tired. I've got this. Trust me."

"Okay, let me know how serious it is."

"Of course! Don't you worry. Love you."

"Love you, too. Bye." She hung up.

Aurel breathed a sigh of relief as he wheezed past the A&E. His destination lay elsewhere.

12

Aurel drove deeper and deeper into the maze of the Orchid Wood. The council forbid public parking in this section of the farm, but Aurel had no choice. He had to get Livie's bleeding body as close as possible to the tunnel without being seen. Luck was on his side—the area seemed deserted. He abandoned the vehicle behind an ancient oak, dragging the child out. Her skin was cold like porcelain. The forest, usually alive with bird songs, was silent as a grave.

Aurel glanced at her peaceful face, seeing a trace of a smile there. He felt jealous. Was she journeying right now in his arms? Through the celestial spheres in the astral plane? "We'll meet again soon, little one. That I promise you."

He slid her body down the muddy path and towards Cornelia's grim residence. His fingers, stained with mud and blood, removed the lock. Aurel swung the gate open. Then he tugged her into the mouth of blackness.

* * * * *

"I see you brought me a present," said Cornelia.

Aurel wiped the sweat off his brow. "Help her, sister! I beg you! Can you help her? I think I stabbed her..."

"Yes, I can help her. *We* can help her together," she said.

Aurel collapsed, his fingernails digging into the dirt. "I can't! I have to get back to Zora! She thinks I'm in a hospital. I need to go home!" He sobbed, broken and defeated.

Cornelia crouched down—her lips close to his ear, hands on his shoulders. "You *are* home, brother."

13

When Zora entered the house, she checked and rechecked her mobile. She called him at frequent intervals, but Aurel's phone was switched off. Why hasn't he called yet? What the fuck was he playing at? She paced back and forth in the living room, sitting down on the sofa, then standing up again. Maternal instinct warned her that something was amiss. She needed a sedative to restrain her anxiety. The decanter full of booze beckoned. She lifted the top and wrapped her lips around the rim, gulping down. It burned in her throat as waves of whiskey dribbled down her chin. The alcohol had the calming effect she desired. Zora picked up her phone again.

Her fingers trembled as she typed the digits. The line rang.

"Medway Maritime Hospital, how can I help?"

"Hello, my name is Zora Schwartz and I'm calling regarding my daughter, Livie. My husband drove her to your hospital, she had a...an accident. A sprained ankle," she said, gulping down more whiskey to steady her voice.

"Livie Schwartz, did you say? Can you hold the line for one minute? I'll check the system to see if your husband brought her in," said the nurse.

Zora raised the decanter back to her lips. Seconds passed like hours.

"Hello? I'm sorry but no one with that name was registered. Are you sure you have the right hospital?"

Zora dropped the phone, crumbling into the sofa. Her mental strength evaporated. The whiskey drowned her common sense. She picked up the phone again, hanging up on the receptionist and dialling Aurel's number.

Voicemail.

"Fuck you!" she shouted, hurling the device at the cushions. *Should I call every hospital in Kent? Where the fuck did you take my daughter?*

Aurel had abandoned her, but so had her wits. Zora picked up her mobile, dialling 999 and pacing around the room. Then she hung up again and slammed it on the table.

Fuck! Why am I calling the coppers? I'm tired and emotional. I'm simply overreacting. Or am I?

Hysterical and confused, Zora snatched the decanter and entered Livie's room. She collapsed on the bed—sniffing and hugging her pillow. The scent of her daughter unleashed a steady stream of tears. She glanced at the pile of clothes, scattered next to the bed.

She squeezed tighter and felt something solid, crushing against her chest. Her curious fingers reached inside the pillowcase and Zora pulled out a simple black notebook. *Livie's diary,* she thought. A pang of guilt struck her as she flipped through the pages. Zora sighed, not wishing to invade her child's privacy but it seemed like a necessary evil. *I have to read it. She might've written something important in there...*

She skipped to the end, reading with bloodshot eyes:

> *Mum must be mental for not noticing! Should I tell her? Or does she know? How could he put his fingers in there! That's so disgusting! How is that even possible? What a bastard. I will tell mum tomorrow.*

Zora re-read the entry several times, tracing each word with her fingertips. She struggled to comprehend Livie's meaning. How could Zora not notice what? Putting his fingers where? What was she talking about? Her brain wrestled with paranoia as she tried to banish thoughts of abuse. *No, he would never lay a finger on Livie. He wouldn't...*

The strain of recent events took a toll on her system. She picked up the decanter next to the bed and drank herself into oblivion.

* * * * *

Darkness had descended outside when Zora peeled her eyes open. Her vision was blurry, her senses still dulled by the liquor. She licked her dehydrated lips and fished the iPhone from the pocket of her jeans. No messages or missed calls from Aurel. The kitchen was crowded by shadows as she drank water from the tap. The torture of not knowing exhausted her all over again. She felt tired, drained. Her previous respite had proved fruitless.

Where could he be? *Where could he possibly take my child? I need to contact his relatives. Maybe they know something. But I never met his fucking relatives! None of them could even be bothered to turn up to our wedding! Not even his estranged mother! Fuck! Why did Eliza push me into online dating that spawned this stupid romance? I should've never listened to her. I only did it to give Livie a real, stable family. How ironic. There are so many missing pieces...*

She closed her eyes, remembering.

"Honestly, creating a profile only takes a minute. You owe it to yourself and Livie. She needs some sort of father figure in her life," Eliza said.

Zora grimaced. "It just seems a bit desperate?"

"Beggars can't be choosers," Eliza laughed, *"and dating sites are full of possibilities—an infinite source of exotic guys,"*

"And perverts and paedophiles," Zora said, nodding.

Eliza waved her hand. "Not all of them. Seriously, give it a shot. Here, give me your phone and I'll snap a few pics for your profile."

"I'm not getting my tits out," Zora said.

"You don't have to. A little cleavage will do."

Fuelled by Eliza's unflinching encouragement, Zora had created a profile on a dating Web site. Messages from some of the most bizarre men in society flooded her inbox within minutes. She scrolled through the obscene messages, regretting participating in this nonsense almost immediately. Then, a photo of an enigmatic man caught her attention. Aurel Schwartz. She gazed into his penetrating eyes, so dark and mysterious, like the waters of Loch Ness she'd visited with Livie a year earlier. She clicked open and began to read:

> *Hello,*
> *Your profile sounds interesting and you seem like a kindred spirit. I'll avoid the usual 'how ARE you?' question which people ask ever so often but rarely mean. How about this instead, what did you have for dinner this evening? Smiley face.*
> *Aurel x*

Zora had grinned. He'd sounded modest and most important of all—normal! She'd expected another pervy message like, "I want to piss in your mouth" or "Tie me to the stove and throw tomatoes at me." Perhaps online dating wasn't so hopeless after all. Zora responded, and they met a week later. She'd never looked back.

Until now.

She began pacing. *His mother—I have to find his mother.* Perhaps he took Livie there? But why would he? And where did she live? Was she local? Or did she live on the other side of the country? Then an idea dawned—Aurel was an avid reader who always scribbled a date and an address into the books he read. He once confessed that he used to move around so much as a youngster, that writing addresses and dates into his books helped him to remember. He said it was like a trip down memory lane every time he picked up an old book that he'd read years ago.

Two pin-pricks of pain flared just behind her eyes, a threatening migraine. Zora rummaged through their bookshelves with purpose, searching for the oldest book in his collection. Her fingers reached for a dusty spine.

The Hobbit—this must be it! He loved it as a child. Said he read the book traditionally every year until his teens.

Eager, she flipped through the pages— hoping she was right.

Isle of Sheppey, Kent, 1972.

14

The Isle of Sheppey was a small island off the northern coast of Kent. Like most people, Zora was familiar with the jibes and jokes involving the island. She'd recently read an article in Kent Online that someone had painted, "Welcome to Hell" on the crossing. Its residents were nicknamed *Swampies*, suggesting that they all had webbed feet and six fingers on each hand. The island was also a home to three prisons. Folks speculated that most islanders resided in one of them.

And then there was the alleged inbreeding.

She only had a partial address, which caused her despair. *What's the population like? These inbreds are supposed to be tight with each other,* she thought, silently laughing at her own joke. *Surely they all know one another in that kind of community?*

Traveling there and asking around was worth a shot. Zora convinced herself that the locals would remember the Schwartz family. She grabbed her purse and keys off the table, ready to drive to the heart of the hellish island.

* * * * *

When she ignited the engine, nothing happened. After several failed attempts, Zora realized that she'd left the headlights on. The battery was flat and she had no idea how to charge it.

Fuck! Why now? Typical luck.

She sat there in silence, thinking. *I'll just have to take a bus. Fuck it. It's not that far from Medway. It'll take ages on the bus. At least 2-3 hours. Still, I need to do this.*

Zora purchased a ticket and rushed through the overcrowded bus station, heading to Bay 14. Whilst waiting for bus 338 to arrive, she contemplated her next move. *When I get there, I'll find a local pub or a café, I guess. They're usually a good source of information. If I'm lucky, someone will point me in the right direction.*

The bus arrived after a twenty-minute delay. She glanced at the side of the vehicle, noticing layers of embedded dirt and grease. She frowned at the filth. How long had it been since she used a public transport? Zora flashed her ticket at the driver who nodded and sat down in the second row.

The journey was long and anxious. A teenage couple sitting behind her cradled a newborn, its screams testing Zora's patience. The sun slipped beyond the horizon, and the bus became a lantern on the dark road. She glimpsed outside only to be greeted by her own reflection.

It dawned on her then that she'd rushed into this—reacting on impulse. She could have called someone about the battery. She could have called on a neighbor. And the island was a dangerous place to be after dark.

The bus halted, and passengers began to disembark. On her way out, Zora stopped by the driver's cabin. "What time is the last bus back?"

The enormous cysts on his neck repulsed her. He glanced at his watch. "In about three hours, lady."

"Cheers," she mumbled, averting her gaze and stepping out into the cold.

* * * * *

The poorly lit bus station casted a vague sphere of light around her, and she was reluctant to leave its protective glow. Other passengers scattered in opposite directions, abandoning her. She scowled. The station appeared to be nothing more than a shack in a middle of deserted country road. Zora pulled the iPhone from her purse. Still no calls or messages from Aurel. She glanced at the sign that displayed *Town Centre*. Turning on the flashlight built inside her mobile, she sighed and marched to the right.

She trekked down a steep hill, flashing light at the hungry darkness. *Fucking great! What was I thinking? Why didn't I wait till the morning before setting out on this wild goose chase? I don't even know where I'm going! Swampies, please don't rape me!*

The arduous descent formed blisters on her heels. To conserve battery life, she switched off the flashlight—until something rustled on her left and she switched it on again with haste. At least her eyes were accustomed to darkness, courtesy of extensive night drives to work. She felt more alert at night, too.

Zora failed to encounter a single soul, but eventually spotted a set of sparkly lights, flickering in the distance. Sweaty feet sprinkled with blisters ached inside her *Rocket Dog* boots. She found herself in the middle of a square. Tall street lamps illuminated her path, so she pocketed her iPhone.

An unfamiliar monument towered over her. Large, spacious houses rested in each direction. The monument concealed a medieval inn. She peered at it and then marched towards *The Headsman* with determination.

On her way in, Zora almost collided with a wooden beam. The old structure had seen better days. She spotted a handful of locals chatting in the corner—all men. The bartender was a handsome chap who greeted her with a polite smile. "Alright, Love? What can I get ya?"

"Just a black coffee, please," Zora replied, surprised by his stunning face. *Where do they keep the freaks then? Perhaps they use his striking good looks to lure people in?*

She slid on a stool by the bar, casting inquisitive glances at her fellow patrons. The pub was entirely lit by candles, cozy and serene. More men drank in the opposite corner. Where were the women? *What is this? Fucking Summerisle?*

The guy served her coffee with shaky hands. She assumed that bartenders had to be confident. So why was this guy so jittery? Or was he on something?

"Thanks," she said. When Zora lifted her gaze, she was met by a flirtatious grin. Perhaps he was confident after all. "Listen," she said. "Could you do me a favour? I'm looking for someone." She leaned toward the fellow, offering a glimpse down her blouse.

"I'll do me best. Who ya after, Love?"

"I'm after my mother-in-law," Zora said.

He reached for a glass and began to polish it with a stained apron that hung by his waist. "I know most of the locals, 'a right bunch of scoundrels I tell ya. What's the name?"

Zora sipped her coffee, disappointed. It tasted like mud. "Schwartz."

"Tamara Schwartz?"

"Possibly. My husband grew up around here and I'm trying to track down his family," she said.

A doddery man approached, asking for another pint. The bartender poured a pint of Doom Bar then passed it to him. "Here we are, Jim."

The old man targeted Zora with his gaze, suspicious.

"Could be her. She's the only Schwartz I know of," said the bartender.

"Sounds like a good enough lead. Do you know where she lives?"

He hesitated. His gaze shifted towards the old man in the corner—towards Jim. "Aye, she lives just around the corner in a tiny cottage."

Zora smiled, leaning forward once more as a gesture of gratitude.
"Would you mind giving me some directions?"

"You can't get lost, Love. Just head back to the Abbey and turn left. It's the fourth cottage down."

Zora checked her iPhone again, crestfallen. Still no message. Glancing up, she said, "Thank you so much for your help."

"Pleasure, Love. Hope you'll find what yer looking for."

15

A mongrel howled somewhere in the distance. How far away, she could not tell. The night-time breeze rustled her hair. She sped towards the cottages, evading shadows. A crunch underfoot made her pause. She lifted her boot, wincing at the ooze. A crushed snail. The grey debris glowed in the moonlight. Zora shuddered when she visualised squashing it—the slimy thing bouncing under her sole like a marshmallow. Bile rose to her throat as she pushed on.

The weather-beaten structures seemed identical, and she counted them with a finger. *One, two, three, four—that must be it.* The brickwork was primitive. She gazed at the cracks in the mortar, and then stepped closer to the window, noticing rot around the wooden frame. A puny light shone within. She knocked on the door, jaw clenched. No response.

The old crone is probably blind and half-deaf.

She sidestepped to the window again, tapping at it with a fingernail. A mosquito buzzed in her right ear and she flinched, waving with both hands. When she turned, a wrinkled face glared at her from the small opening. Zora yelped, retreating.

Years hadn't been kind to the woman. Her hollow eyes were like black caves, her nose bumpy and covered in warts. A grin stretched across her paper-thin lips. The woman raised a finger, a signal to wait. Zora nodded at the crusty face.

"Who are yer? What do yer want?" asked the old woman, revealing half a face.

Zora attempted a polite smile, but it was lost in the dark. "I'm sorry to bother you so late, but I'm looking for Tamara Schwartz. My name is Zora. Zora Schwartz. I'm her daughter-in-law."

"Eh? Yer after Tamara?"

"Yes, do you know her?"

The woman's shrivelled mouth and sunken cheeks hinted at absent teeth. She glared with suspicion but then her eyes softened. "Aye, I know 'er. Yer best come in." She beckoned inside, slamming the wobbly door behind them.

Zora followed her into a humble room, shrouded in dim light. The old woman limped with a permanent hunch, pale and fragile like a withering tree. Zora glanced at the furnishings, simple yet elegant. A hand-carved table nestled by the east wall. A single bed protruded from the left, and a Gothic-style wardrobe guarded the back of the dwelling.

"Would yer like some tea?"

"Yes, that would be lovely, thank you. If you show me where the kitchen is, I'll make it and save you the trouble." Zora offered.

"Don't be daft! I'm stronger than I look. And I'm Tamara, by the way. 'Ere, have a seat." She pointed at an uncomfortable chair and disappeared into the kitchenette around the corner.

"Oh! Pleasure to meet you at last," Zora said to an empty wall. "I'm sorry to barge in on you like this, but I really need to speak to you about your son,"

"Nah, don't yer worry 'bout it. We're tough 'round 'ere, yer know? I can handle m'self just fine."

Restless, Zora crept into the kitchenette. She was eager to gaze into Tamara's face. Lies flowed easily when separated by a wall. Her eyes would know the difference—or so she hoped.

Lifting the kettle required concentration on Tamara's part, and her hands trembled as she poured boiling water into ceramic mugs. Zora noticed embedded limescale at the base of the kettle and wondered when it was last cleaned.

"Please, allow me to carry the tray at least," she said.

The woman nodded, clearing her throat with a raspy cough. They sat down, and Zora dropped two sugar cubes into her mug. She sighed.

"I don't even know where to begin," she said, massaging the bridge of her nose. "My daughter, Livie, sprained her ankle, and Aurel was supposed to drive her to a hospital, you. But he switched off his phone, and I can't reach him. I called our local hospital, but they had no record of her. They've been missing for almost two days now. I was hoping you'd be able to help."

Tamara listened, sipping her tea with an irritating slurp. Their gazes collided—Zora's moist with tears, and Tamara's black as coal.

"Nah, he didn't take yer girl to no hospital." Tamara said, draining her cup. "Yer don't know much about me son, do yer? Silly mare. 'Ere, I'll pour yer another cup of tea and I'll tell yer bout him." She lifted the pot.

16

"Aurel always was a...what yer call it? A *unique* child," Tamara Schwartz said, clicking her fingers. "A *rare breed*, if yer like. He began sleepwalking when he was a wee boy. Frightened the livin' hell outta us! We dragged him to all kinds of doctors, but they never did nout. His father used to say that the boy was cursed. He never did have much love for him, me husband. Aye, a difficult brat to raise, Aurel was. 'Ere on the island, the parents raise their sprogs freely, yer know? We 'ave soft hearts and let 'em do what they want. Aurel was an outdoor brat, like most chaps 'round 'ere, bunking school and the like. Then one day, me husband slapped him for stealing, and the boy ran from home. We made nout of it, yer know? Figurin' he crashed over at a neighbour's house or somethin'."

"Why did he run away? Because he stole, and your husband struck him, did you say?" Zora asked, struggling to interpret the woman's Sheppey drawl.

Tamara lowered her weary gaze, blood rushing into her cheeks. Zora wondered if she blushed from anger or embarrassment. "Nah, not because of the stealin', although steal he did. Many times, yer know? Nah, that had nout to do with it."

The old woman took a deep breath. "There was somethin' else. Me late husband, Alexander, abused the boy for years. Sexually, if yer catch me drift? Aye, it ain't easy to talk 'bout. I swear to yer, I didn't know! Aurel was always a rascal, but started actin' weird, as yer can imagine. He stopped talkin' to me and other kids, isolating himself like. Pete, one of me neighbour's kids, bumped into me one mornin', sayin' that he saw Aurel bunkin' in some dirty tunnel, playin' with dolls. I just shook me head, letting the boy to his own devices, yer know?" The old woman paused to take another sip. "Me husband died soon after, and Aurel returned. We got pissed on cider at the funeral an' he rambled on 'bout the abuse. I slapped him. Didn't believe a word! But maybe it was true, yer know?"

Zora glared at the woman, struggling to contain her judgement. What kind of mother was she? Abandoning her abused child like that? *Poor Aurel.* She began to understand his need for a normal family, and why he severed ties, erasing these people from his memory. They were no family. They were less than human.

"So he just left for good after the funeral? You never once tried to make amends?" Zora asked, her words sprinkled with bitterness.

"Whatcha take me for? I'm old, yer know? I always *felt* old. I had no energy like to gallop after him. He knew where I was, yeah? If he wanted to 'ave a chat, all he had to do was come back. I ain't goin' nowhere.

The lack of empathy shocked her. Zora's dislike for the woman began to show in her demeanor. She twitched in her seat, agitated. These disturbing revelations fuelled her paranoia, and she began to wonder if she ever really knew her husband—his true feelings and desires. What he was capable of. What would he sacrifice for her? For Livie? She despaired at the mere fragments of his persona he chose to reveal. What else lurked beneath the surface? What else did he hide from them?

Tamara's cough sliced her thoughts in half. "Hope you 'ave a strong stomach coz there's somethin' else he probably failed to tell yer."

"Oh, really? And what may that be?" Zora asked, impatient with the woman's condescending attitude.

"The folks 'round 'ere never heard of this word, but I bet a sophisticated lass like yerself 'ave."

"Which word?" Zora said, raising an eyebrow.

Tamara slurped from her cup, tea dribbling down her saggy skin. "*Chimera.*"

The word struck a chord.

"Chimera? You mean the monstrous, fire-breathing hybrid from Greek Mythology?" she asked, perplexed.

Tamara's chuckle resonated in the room. "Nah, yer mong. A *human* Chimera. 'Ave yer heard of it?"

"No, what is it?"

Tamara pulled a note from the pocket of her apron and snatched her glasses off the shelf. Then she began to read.

A Chimera *is a single organism composed of genetically distinct*

*cells. This can result in male and
female organs or two different
blood types. In layman terms, yer
one person outside but two people
inside.*

The stained note slipped from her fingers
and drifted underneath the table. Tamara
studied her with a curious expression.

Zora's face turned pale. "What? Are you
saying that Aurel is a human Chimera? That he
has *both* male and female genitals?" She
pondered for a moment. "I think you're confusing
Chimera with Hermaphrodite. Is that what—"

Zora froze, recalling Livie's strange diary
entry. *Mum must be mental for not noticing!
Should I tell her? Or does she know? How could
he put his fingers in there! That's so disgusting!
How is that even possible?*

The missing pieces fell into place. *She
must've seen him pleasuring his...what? His
vagina?* "This is absurd. I'd have noticed."

Tamara shrugged her flimsy shoulders.
"Yer can't see it easily. It's hidden below his
scrotum like. But aye, he was born with one
testicle, an ovary, and a fallopian tube."

Zora rubbed her forehead in frustration.
*What the fuck? My husband is a Hermaphrodite?
Or something more? With two different types of
DNA? What did she say? A human Chimera? For
Christ's sake! What kind of freak have I married?
I knew he only had one testicle—he said that
much. But a fallopian tube as well?*

She felt dizzy, shocked by another sudden

realization. *That's why he never turned on the lights when we were having sex. That's why he never let me go down on him. I should've known something was wrong. I'm so stupid!*

Zora felt anger rise in her voice. "So where is he now then?"

"Yer know bloody well where he is! Try the nearest tunnel 'round yer house. I bet he took 'er there for picnic or somethin'."

Zora tapped on the edge of the table with her nails. "With a sprained ankle? Why would he do that?"

"Find him yerself then if yer don't believe me, but I'm telling yer—that's where they'll be."

She nodded, eager to leave immediately. "Thank you so much for your hospitality and all your help, *Mrs. Schwartz.*"

Tamara waved her hand, disturbing a moth that flew towards the light. "Nah, don't mention it. It was 'bout time we met, eh? Yer like me daughter now," she said, caressing Zora's cheek with a calloused palm.

Zora pulled away. She paused in the doorframe, sliding the strap of her handbag further up. "Once we clear up this confusion, I'll have a word with Aurel. I'm sure he'd love to see his mother again," she said. The tone of her voice said otherwise.

Tamara flashed a smile burdened with sorrow. "That bridge has already been burned, yer know? But yer welcome to try."

17

Zora tripped in the dark, cursing, but regained her balance almost instantly. Tail lights shone in the distance, and Zora sprinted towards the bus—puffing. *Wait for me, you bastard! I don't want to be stuck in this shithole overnight!* When she boarded, the repulsive cysts of the driver greeted her. *Oh, God! Not him again. Can this night get any worse?* Zora flashed her ticket and sped past the rows of empty seats, shaking her head at all the rubbish people left behind. She nestled into a seat at the far back. The doors shut and her eyes with them.

Zora mulled over Tamara's words but the brash sound of the engine disrupted her concentration. *I still don't believe half of what that old bitch had said. Let's face it, she was senile and thick—clearly not giving a toss about her son. But on the other hand, why would she lie?*

The iPhone vibrated in her pocket and she whipped it out, eyes alert and heart racing. She scoffed and deleted the spam e-mail with a swipe of her finger.

Plan your funeral for as little as £2.86 a month, indeed.

* * * * *

The door creaked as she nudged it with her shoulder. She flipped on the light switch in the hallway, listening. The house was devoid of life. Zora glanced at the walls in Livie's room. They were plastered with tender memories. She missed her daughter's laugh. The way her eyes lit up with that childish enthusiasm. *Where can they be? Where did you take her?*

A tunnel, his mother had said. *Aurel did mention a tunnel once, somewhere on Capstone Farm but I was barely listening at the time. Could Tamara be right? Did he take Livie there? But why? And with a busted ankle? It just doesn't add up. Something's wrong. But I have to entertain every possibility. I have to find them!*

She rummaged in the cupboard and grinned in triumph at the robust flashlight. *I can't rely on my mobile, the battery is almost dead and I don't have time to charge it right now. What else will I need?* Her eyes rested on a small retractable knife. She hesitated, but stashed it inside the back pocket of her jeans. *So many creepy cunts around here, especially in the middle of the night. I'll feel safer with it.* The possibility of using the weapon against Aurel crossed her mind like a bullet. *No, he wouldn't hurt Livie. He loves her. But what about me? Does he love me?* Zora pulled a hoody over her head, smoothing out the creases with her palms. In need of liquid courage, she gulped down the last of the whiskey and stepped out into the night.

* * * * *

An ailing yellow glow shone from the streetlights as she walked briskly down Luton Road—the dodgiest road in Chatham. She kept her eyes on the pavement, face half concealed under the hood. A group of young chavs socialized outside the kebab shop, and she crossed the road just to avoid any hassle. Luton Road was populated with *To Let* signs, as no decent family wished to live there. The neighborhood was a human skip. Zora turned into Capstone Road and paced for another twenty-five minutes.

To my advantage, I know Capstone like the back of my hand. My parents dragged me there practically every weekend during the summer. Now let's see, that tunnel he mentioned, where could it be? Think! It can't be anywhere near Maze Wood. That's where the fishing lake is, and there are always people about. Where else? Orchid Wood? Possibly. There's not much there, just muddy paths and overgrown bushes. Hold on! I swear there was a tunnel or bunker or something like that down there! Karen and I found it when we were kids. It's the only one I can think of. Now where was it exactly?

She crossed the field in pitch black, petrified to turn on her flashlight and attract attention. What if someone trolled Capstone at night? The waning moon illuminated her steps as she followed intuition along a path constructed by memories. She found herself surrounded by trees. Zora pressed the button and the light trembled in her hand. She flashed it at the shrubs. In between, behind the oak, the rays of light glimmered over a silver surface. *That's his fucking car! They're here! I found them!*

Adrenaline sharpened her senses as she approached the vehicle. It was abandoned. *The tunnel is close. I recognise this place, even at witching hour.* She kicked aside a pile of dead leaves and gazed at the gap, leading further down. A discarded copy of *The Guardian* bathed in a shallow sewage sludge. Then she glimpsed the arch. Someone attempted to disguise the entrance with lanky branches, but it was a poor effort. Zora swung them aside, fingering the chain. The lock hung loose, as did her jaw. *Why did he bring Livie here? Into this putrid hellhole?* Her stomach knotted at the thought. She clasped one of the steel handles and yanked. The strain screamed in her shoulder and lower back. *Fucking hell! That was heavy! Glad I'm working out and have the strength to move this fucking thing.*

She flashed the beam within, directing light at dripping walls. *This ends here.*

18

The place was a cold tomb, and she trembled from the sudden temperature shift. A drop of water landed on her neck, prickling her skin. She treaded with caution, peering at the deformed bricks. A flame flickered in the corner of her peripheral vision and she veered left. The light of her torch exposed a narrow cavity in the wall. Then a crunch. Zora cursed under her breath when she realised another snail lay dead beneath her boot.

"I knew you'd find me," said the voice from within the cavity. "I'm so happy you've decided to join us at last."

Her knees wobbled and she supressed a scream. A table constructed out of bricks and a wooden board lay in the corner. On top, a cocktail of various chemicals and surgical instruments. Her gaze shifted towards a life-size doll sitting in a broken chair. She blinked and gasped. The mummified cadaver belonged to a young girl. Tears spilled when she gazed at Aurel, kneeling beside another body—her daughter's body—

washing her corpse with a soaked cloth. Words failed her.

"You have no idea how glad I am that you're here," Aurel said, wiping under Livie's armpits with the cloth. "It's such a relief! My sister was dying to meet you. We can be a proper family with no more secrets between us."

She found her voice and kicked the table in primal rage. "You sick *cunt*! What the *fuck* have you done? You don't even have a sister!"

Aurel flashed a sly grin. "Oh, but I do. I'm just very protective of her. But she warned me this would happen eventually. Isn't that right, Cornelia?"

She followed his glance towards an empty mattress, stained with delusion.

"Who are you talking to, Aurel? There's no one there!"

He kept his gaze on Livie's milky thighs, washing them with tenderness. "Reveal yourself to my beloved wife, Cornelia. Don't be afraid. There's no need for secrecy any longer."

Zora clenched her jaw, Tamara's words surging through her brain. She crouched down. "Listen to me very carefully, Aurel. I spoke to your mother and she told me everything. *There is no Cornelia.*"

Aurel's washcloth dropped like a guillotine. "You what? You spoke to...Tamara? Why? What lies did she tell you?"

"She told me *everything*. About your father's abuse, too. What was his name, Alexander?"

The name squeezed his face purple and his lips curled with contempt.

"Tamara also told me about your tunnels and where to find you. And one more thing," Zora said, brushing away tears. "She said you're a human chimera. A freak of nature! Born with a cock *and* a cunt! But that's not all! If she's right, you have two different blood types! Do you know what that means? It means you have a twin trapped *inside* of you, Aurel. Cornelia never existed in the real world—"

Aurel patted his chest, struggling to breathe. "You lie! Cornelia! Confess! Tell her everything!"

"There's no one there, you sick fuck! No! Don't touch her! Get away from *my daughter!*" Zora watched him retreat on the mattress like a cornered beast.

"You lie! You lie! *You lie!*"

Zora knelt beside Livie, stroking her hair matted with blood. "I'm so sorry I've failed you!" She wailed, clutching Livie to her breast.

Aurel rocked on the mattress, hands wrapped around his knees. "You lying cunt! What are you doing? Don't you *understand?* I just wanted a proper family. Livie saw Cornelia and I making love, and I couldn't risk her revealing my secret. But now you know. You know! And there's nothing left to hide."

He rose and walked to her, fingers outstretched. In a moment, he was choking her. She wiggled on the ground, grasping for the knife hidden in her pocket. A shift in momentum allowed her to shove him aside. Survival instinct and adrenaline fuelled her strength. She swung in a vicious arc, the tip of the blade catching his cheek and slashing it open. Aurel staggered, stricken with panic.

Zora screamed. "All she saw was you fucking *yourself!* There is no Cornelia! You killed my daughter because..." She waved the knife in warning. "Because she saw what a *freak* you are!"

Before she could react, Aurel rugby tackled her to the ground—pinning her arms with his knees and snatching the knife from her grasp. In dominant rage, he pushed back her forehead, exposing her swan-like neck, and with one fluid motion, slashed her throat. A geyser of blood painted his face red. Aurel yelled, victorious.

She lay gurgling on the ground, staring into his eyes.

"It will be over soon," he said, panting and stroking her hair.

19

Once their cadavers were washed, he began the drainage. He bled Livie's feeble frame first before injecting a mixture of formaldehyde, glutaraldehyde, and methanol into her arterial system.

"What madness!" he muttered. "How dare she deny your existence? You should've spoken with her, Cornelia, but I forgive your shyness." Aurel continued pumping chemicals into his stepdaughter, stopping only to massage her body in order to break up any circulatory clots. With the draining complete, he rewashed her corpse and moved on to Zora.

The embalming processes lasted for hours, and his fingers ached. He collapsed on the mattress and admired his art, savouring every moment. Then he groomed their bodies and applied moisturising cream.

"Look at our family, Cornelia. Don't they seem livelier than ever?"

* * * * *

Dawn greeted him when he emerged from the tunnel. The area seemed deserted still as he folded the backseats to create more transporting room. Aurel checked for prying eyes before loading the cadavers. The dead weight of Zora's beefy body almost buckled his knees. He strapped them in. Then he remembered the cut on his cheek. It still bled a little. Uncapping a bottle, he splashed water on his face before fishing out the first aid kit from the glove compartment. He scrubbed bits of dry blood off his face and slicked back his hair before glancing at his family from the rear-view mirror.

"You might have to hold them, Cornelia. The trail gets bumpy in the woods."

20

Gravel crunched under the rubber as he pulled outside the cottage. The door was unlocked and he collected tools and chemicals from the car, dragging them inside his childhood home.

"What's for tea, Ma? I'm starving!"

Tamara Schwartz limped from the kitchen, extending her frail arms. She embraced her son, planting a kiss on his uncut cheek.

"Yer favourite, me lad! Bangers n' mash. I'll heat it up for you! 'Ere, sit yerself down an' tell me all 'bout it. Is it done? Are they 'ere like?"

The chair scraped against the wood as he sat down, rolling up his sleeves. "Yep, it went pretty smooth! Exactly as you planned, Ma. They're waiting in the car now. We'll all be reunited at last. One big happy family. Is Dad downstairs?"

She slid a steaming plate under his nose and Aurel salivated.

"Aye, he's waitin' for you all downstairs. We'll pop down when yer finish yer tea. Eat up!"

He bit into the sausage, juices splashing on his stubble.

* * * * *

"Zora and Livie are so excited about meeting Dad! They've been looking forward to it for such a long time!" Aurel said, descending the stairs into the crypt-like bedroom below. Tamara nodded behind him, a set of keys chimed in her wrinkled hands. She unlocked the chamber and his gaze rested on a familiar painting, hanging above the bed. He traced the lines with the tip of his finger. A Negress, chained to the sacrificial alter dominated the centre. A figure cloaked in black leaned over her naked body, arms outstretched. Transparent male figures guarded all four corners whilst a miniature dragon-like silhouette crept up the stairs leading up to the altar. Aurel glanced at the flaming chalice, burning in the background. The relevance of the paining died with his father. Now it was a piece of mysterious nostalgia. He studied the circular room and the quartet of empty beds around him. The stench wriggled his nose. Sitting on the edge of the fifth bed, he gazed at the stiff face.

"Hello, Da. It's so good to see you again. I brought you a surprise. Do you remember when you told me that I was incapable of starting a family of my own? That no one would ever love me? Well, you were *wrong*. I have a wife and a daughter. They're here, eager to meet you. Does that please you? Are you proud of me? I'm not your little disappointment now, am I?"

Tamara ushered him out. "No time fer idle chit chat! Bring yer family down 'ere an' I'll make tea."

* * * * *

The porcelain-like faces glared at him, even from the afterlife. He'd dressed them in satin, pearl white dresses that radiated ethereal beauty.

"Yer chose well, me lad. Yer Da is proud of yer. As am I." Tamara lowered her teacup into the chipped saucer.

Aurel nodded, still captivated. "Thanks, Ma. This is a historic moment. All of us together for the first time. Me, Zora, Livie, Cornelia, you and Da. Such a magical blessing."

"Aye, it's nearly over. Are you ready, me lad?"

He grinned, nearly drowning in joy. "Yes, Ma. Let me bathe and then we shall begin."

* * * * *

Tamara watched her son as he slid into the bathtub, water spilling over the edges. He caught a glimpse of her before the mirror steamed up.

"Will you bathe me, Ma?"

She nodded, snatching a clean cloth from a cupboard below the sink.

"Relax," she said, gripping his shoulder and pulling back.

Aurel obliged, as any good son should. She soaped the cloth and began scrubbing his chest and arms, then back. His mind wandered and he fantasized about the astral plane. Would they embrace him as a brother? The ethereal beings? He moaned when Tamara washed the tip of his penis, his bollocks and the foreskin. She gently lifted his scrotum and cleaned the small slit beneath it. The palm of her hand pressed against his head and he submerged. The shampoo smelled of coconut as she massaged it into his scalp. Then he rinsed it out.

"Yer ready? Everythin' is prepared."

He grinned, sliding a stiff towel off the rack. Once dried, Aurel entered the family room and nestled into the vacant bed next to his father. He glanced at the surgical steel, sprawled on a stool. The instrument felt cold against his skin.

"Let the bloodletting commence," he said, jabbing the needle into his basilic vein. The blood dripped into the silver bowl below in a steady rhythm.

"Will you join me shortly, Ma?"

"I'll be right behind yer, don't yer worry."

About the Author

Erik Hofstatter is a schlock horror writer and a member of the *Horror Writers Association*. Born in the wild lands of the Czech Republic, he roamed Europe before subsequently settling on English shores, studying creative writing at the London School of Journalism. He now dwells in Kent, where he can be encountered consuming copious amounts of mead and tyrannizing local peasantry. His other works include *The Pariahs, Amaranthine and Other Stories, Katerina,* and *Moribund Tales.* He can be followed using the following links:

Web site: www.erikhofstatter.net
Twitter and Instagram: @ErikHofstatter
Facebook:
www.facebook.com/erkhofstatter

About the Artist

Jack Larson is a self-taught artist who has been painting and selling macabre art since 2009. Although he began painting as a teenager, he didn't take it seriously as an occupation, and instead enlisted in the U.S. Army immediately after high school. His training as a Mortuary Affairs Specialist prepared him for a decade long career in the death-care profession, which included embalming, decedent transportation, and homicide cleanup. The years he spent away from art prepared him for the business side of being an artist, as well as providing him with the experiences and sights that inspire his work today.

6021 Obenchain Rd.

Laporte, Colorado
80535

Rare Breeds
A Dark Silo Press Book / October 2016
Copyright 2016 / Dark Silo Press / All rights
reserved

Illustrations: Jack Larson
Cover Design: Jessica Babb-Raymundo
Interior Design: Brian Kaufman
Editorial Assistance: Jamie Schenkel

eBook Design by
52 Novels